PUDDING
BAG
SCHOOL

* * * * * * *

Cold Enough
For Snow

For more about the author visit:
www.hilarymckay.co.uk

Read more Pudding Bag School adventures:

The Birthday Wish
A Strong Smell of Magic

By the same author:

Saffy's Angel
(Winner of the Whitbread Children's Book Award)
Indigo's Star
Permanent Rose
Caddy Ever After
Forever Rose

The Exiles
(Winner of the Guardian Children's Fiction Award)
The Exiles at Home
The Exiles in Love

Rescuing Robin
The Chickenpox Club

Happy and Glorious
Practically Perfect

Paradise House Series:
The Zoo in the Attic
The Treasure in the Garden
The Echo in the Chimney
The Magic in the Mirror
The Surprise Party
Keeping Cottontail

HILARY McKAY

PUDDING BAG SCHOOL

Cold Enough for Snow

Hodder
Children's
Books

A division of Hachette Children's Books

To Kimberly, Kayleigh and Laura Iles,
with love

CHAPTER ONE
Dinner Ladies' Detention

On the day that the weather finally became
cold enough for snow, Class 4b, Pudding Bag
School, were given dinner ladies' detention.
Nobody escaped. Dinner that day had been
Mock Cod Pie and Class 4b had refused to
eat it.

"And it was delicious beautiful home
cooking," said Mrs Muldoon, the chief dinner
lady. "The finest fish!"

"In a light cheese sauce," chimed in
Miss Spigot, the second dinner lady. "With
a mashed potato top."

"And padding!"

That was Amelia Pilchard, the third and last dinner lady. Mrs Muldoon was large and purple and Miss Spigot was bony and blue, but Amelia Pilchard blended into the landscape like fog. Miss Pilchard was a padding expert. That meant she was very good indeed at mixing extra and unexpected ingredients into recipes, in order to make them go further.

"Perhaps it was the padding that caused the problems," suggested Miss Gilhoolie, Class 4b's teacher, when she heard about her class's refusal to eat.

"It was wonderful padding," said Mrs Muldoon. "You could never have told it wasn't natural! The problem was caused by that redheaded Dougal McDougal! He started them all off, hiccuping and choking and making remarks!"

This sounded more than likely to Miss

Gilhoolie. She knew Dougal McDougal very well indeed. He was very often the beginning of trouble. So she sighed but said to Mrs Muldoon, "In that case I suppose detention it must be. Poor dears! I will let their families know you are keeping them at school."

That was how Class 4b came to be alone in Pudding Bag School with nobody with them but the three dinner ladies. That was where they were when the first snowflake fell.

Nobody noticed it. It vanished before it touched the ground.

But it was the first of millions.

Dinner ladies' detention took place in the dining hall, a high-windowed, echoing and very chilly place. Class 4b were given paper and pencils and the menu board to copy out twenty times each as punishment, and the dinner ladies left them to huddle in the warmth of the cleaners' cupboard.

Simon Percy, who kept a diary, copied down the menu from the menu board as Madeline Brown read it out.

MOCK COD PIE / MILD MIXED ROOT CURRY

RUSSIAN TRIFLE / JELLY SURPRISE
All made from the finest ingredients

"All made from the *same* ingredients!" commented Dougal McDougal. "The only difference between the trifle and the pie was that one had bits of beetroot and the other had bits of fish. And the jelly had beetroot in as well."

"The trifle," remarked Simon, "had mashed potato on it! Lend me a line-writer somebody!"

Line-writers had been invented by Madeline Brown, the school brain, and manufactured by

Mr Bedwig, ex-caretaker. You slid your paper into a wooden frame and a simple mechanism of cogs and levers allowed ten pencils to write at once. Simon was handed half a dozen line writers by people who had already completed their twenty of the menu board.

"I do miss Mr Bedwig," he remarked, as he set to work, and there was a murmur of agreement from all around. Mr Bedwig had worked at Pudding Bag School the term before and no caretaker could have been more useful. He had actually helped Class 4b build a rocket that had successfully blasted their frightful headmaster into space. The rocket had been designed by Madeline, but it had been Mr Bedwig who collected most of the parts and carried out the actual welding. Also, he had brought home Simon Percy's long-lost parents, redecorated the entire school, installed solar panels on the roof and an escape tunnel in the basement, banished chewing gum for ever, and adopted a cat.

Then, when everyone was just settling down to live happily ever after, he had announced that he was needed elsewhere, and vanished.

"At least he left the cat," said Madeline. The cat, Bagdemagus, was curled up on her lap. He was the warmest thing in the school. "I wonder ..."

Right in the middle of Madeline's wonder the dining-hall door was pushed open and Kate McDougal, Dougal's eighteen-year-old sister, blew into the room. Dougal had seven older sisters. Kate was his favourite. She was the youngest and prettiest and kindest, and by far the most excitable. Right now she was glowing with cold and excitement.

"What are you all doing, still at school?" she demanded. "Darling Dougal, I brought your wellies! Hadn't you better come home straight away? I've never seen such snow!"

"Snow!" shrieked Class 4b in delight, and there was an immediate rush to the windows.

"Up to my knees," Kate told them. "And drifting already. Didn't you notice?"

"No," said Dougal. "We've been doing dinner ladies' detention. We can't go home yet either, we've got another half hour. We've to write out the menu twenty times each. We've been using Mr Bedwig's line-writing machines."

"Mr Bedwig was a poppet," remarked Kate, perching herself on a windowsill and swinging her legs. "I wonder how he's getting on at the zoo."

Line-writing, dinner ladies and even the knee-high snow outside were forgotten in the buzz of excitement that followed.

"What's he doing at the zoo?"

"Caretaking of course," said Kate.

"How do you know?"

"I saw him."

"Why didn't you tell anyone?"

"I didn't think to," said Kate. "I didn't know you didn't know. I saw him when I went to say goodbye."

"Goodbye to Mr Bedwig?"

"Goodbye to the animals. They're being moved. Sent home most of them. Not the cold weather ones. They're staying where they are with Mr Bedwig."

"But why?"

"Because of the weather forecast," explained Kate patiently. "You know. Flooding. Arctic freezes. Lots of snow. They've been saying it all winter."

"It never comes, though," said Dougal.

"It's here now," said Kate cheerfully. "Coming down in bucketfuls! And the Thames burst its banks this morning, and then froze. Solid ice, South London is, all the way to Kent!"

This was very exciting news. At the beginning of winter exactly such weather had been forecast. People had laid in huge supplies of food and books and candles. Travel agents had made fortunes selling holidays in the winter sun. Thermal underwear and knitted woolly hats had come back into fashion.

Then December had arrived and been the warmest on record and people began to feel a little foolish.

January was the first frost-free January in living memory.

In the first week of February the daffodils came out. They had never been so early.

"Global warming," people said gloomily as they packed away their thermal vests and woolly hats and candles.

No sooner had they finished than it began to rain. Six months supply of rain fell in two days, the daffodils were washed away, and an icy wind began to blow from the North.

"And now look at it!" said Kate.

Class 4b, with their noses pressed to the cold glass of the dining-room windows, looked. The world outside was a tumbling blur of snowflakes. It really was, as Kate had said, coming down in bucketfuls.

"Hurray!" said Dougal. "We've never had real proper snow before."

As he spoke a gust of wind hit the window so hard that it burst open. Blinding whiteness filled the room, every piece of paper went flying, aching cold attacked from all sides and a deep howling echoed through the room. Madeline, and half a dozen people after her, flung themselves at the window and wrestled it shut. Then the white cloud cleared and the howling diminished and Class 4b were left staring at each other in shocked amazement.

"Good job I brought your wellies," said Kate

to Dougal, but she sounded a little uncertain as she said it. She could not help wondering if wellies would be enough to make sure that Dougal got safely home that night. And even if they were, worried Kate, what about the rest of Class 4b? Most of them were considerably smaller and much less tough than her brother.

It was Madeline who said aloud what Kate was thinking.

"We shan't get home in that," said Madeline.

The noise when the dining-room window blew open had penetrated even to the cleaners' cupboard.

"How those kiddies do howl!" remarked Miss Spigot, as she dunked her sixth custard cream in her mug of hot chocolate.

"Stomach ache," said Mrs Muldoon wisely. "Martyrs to it, children are. Mine were all exactly the same."

Amelia Pilchard tittered silently.

"All six," continued Mrs Muldoon. "Terrible groaners, till the end."

"The end?" queried Miss Spigot softly, sensing tragedy.

"Took off," said Mrs Muldoon, not softly at all, and there was a general tutting of disapproval in the cleaning cupboard.

"Never wrote?" asked Miss Spigot, after a suitable pause.

"Not a line," replied Mrs Muldoon "There's no gratitude in this world for those that bring up children."

There was a lot of solemn nodding in the cupboard. The sounds from the dining hall died away with the closing of the window and there was nothing to be heard but the shuffle of biscuits in the biscuit tin as Amelia Pilchard poked through the top layers in search of the broken fragments underneath.

"There's no gratitude in the world at all, if you ask me," remarked Miss Spigot. "Look at us! Where would they be without us dinner ladies, and yet never a word of thanks!"

"We should get medals for all the years we've done!"

"Honoured by the nation for feeding the nation's kiddies!"

"Footballers get knighthoods, just for kicking a ball around!"

"They don't give ladies knighthoods," said Miss Spigot. "What do they get instead?"

"They make 'em Dames," said Mrs Muldoon. "I should just fancy being a Dame! Dame Lacey Muldoon!"

"Dame Pansy Spigot!" said Miss Spigot. "Ooooh, how gorgeous!"

"Dame Amelia Pilchard!" said Amelia Pilchard. "Perfect in every way!"

They sighed and smiled at the lovely

thought, and then they passed round the biscuit tin again.

Back in the dining room Class 4b were still watching the storm outside the windows. It was getting worse and worse.

"I wonder if those dinner ladies of yours know about this weather," said Kate suddenly. "I'm going to find them!" And she went and hammered on the cleaning-cupboard door.

The dinner ladies were terribly concerned when they heard about the snow. They hurried to the dining room and peered out of the windows. Every moment the blizzard was blowing more strongly. The glass shook and rattled in the gale.

The dinner ladies looked at each other, and then they looked at Class 4b and they said almost exactly what Madeline had said earlier.

"They'll never get home in that!"

"I'm sure you are right," agreed Kate. "I think that most of them would blow away. You three might manage it, I suppose."

This was true. Mrs Muldoon with her bulk and her zip-up fleece-lined boots might make it home. So might Miss Spigot, built as she was like animated scaffolding. So might Amelia Pilchard, who although she did not look it, was the toughest of them all, but ...

"Leave the kiddies!" cried Miss Spigot. "Never!"

"Here we stay," agreed Miss Pilchard.

"It is our duty," said Mrs Muldoon.

Then for the first time it dawned on Class 4b that they were there for the night – stuck in Pudding Bag School in the middle of a blizzard with the three dinner ladies for comfort. Samantha Freebody shivered and sniffed, Emma and Charlotte, the identical twins, burst into identical tears, and several people began to look very alarmed.

"Stop it, please stop it!" begged Kate, with her hands over her ears. "It might just be till evening. The snow could stop any minute."

"It's up to the windowsills now," said Simon.

"It's nearly dark," said Madeline.

"I'm terribly hungry," said Dougal McDougal, and immediately wished he hadn't because the dinner ladies looked at each other and said, "Supper!"

"Darling Mrs Muldoon," said Kate, who had heard many stories about the dinner ladies' cooking from Dougal. "Please don't bother about supper!"

But Mrs Muldoon and her assistants would not hear of not bothering. Cooking was their duty, they said, and cook they would. They said it would be a disgrace if they didn't. They grew quite excited at the thought. There was not much in, they told Kate, but nothing to stop them having a rake around.

"Soup," said Miss Pilchard. "Soup's a treat for adding padding."

"Dumplings in it," said Miss Spigot. "All kiddies love dumplings."

"Hot milk and bicarb," said Mrs Muldoon. "All my six had hot milk and bicarb at bedtime. Sent them off proper!"

With that all three dinner ladies marched to the kitchen.

"Who would have thought they would be so kind?" exclaimed Kate, not knowing the little song that was already beginning in each dinner lady's head.

"Dame Lacey Muldoon!"

"Dame Pansy Spigot!"

"Dame Amelia Pilchard!"

"Kind!" groaned Dougal McDougal when the dinner ladies had gone. "You won't say that when you taste their cooking! I'm not sure I can bear it twice in one day! We've already had to cope with Mock Cod Pie."

"Think about something else," said Kate briskly. "If we have to stay here, where had it better be? Where would you like to sleep?"

"Not in the dining room," said Simon Percy.

"Nor with the dinner ladies," said Dougal McDougal.

"No, no," agreed everyone at once. "Definitely not with the dinner ladies!"

In the kitchen the dinner ladies were also discussing where they would spend the night.

"Definitely not with the kiddies!" called Miss Spigot through clouds of steam, and Mrs Muldoon and Amelia Pilchard nodded in agreement.

"Cooking, yes," said Mrs Muldoon. "That I will undertake. But sleeping with the little horro— dears. No! They will be up and down all night, and there would not be a minute's peace."

"Besides, they won't be alone," said Miss Spigot. "They've got Young Kate. How's the soup, Amelia dear?"

"Thickening beautifully," crooned Amelia Pilchard, scooping dollops of mashed potato into a simmering vat of tap water. "Time for the dumplings!"

"Lovely, lovely dumplings!" sang Miss Spigot as she swayed across the kitchen with an enormous tray full of floury balls that shone with a pale and greenish light.

"Parsley?" enquired Mrs Muldoon.

"That cabbage they never ate Thursday," Miss Spigot told her.

"Tuesday," said Miss Pilchard.

"Tuesday then. Chopped it up and popped it in. Waste not, want not."

"Set 'em up perfect for the night," said Mrs

Muldoon cheerfully. "Knock 'em out, so to speak! And as for us, I thought we might tuck up in here. Leave on the gas oven and fetch in the staff-room armchairs."

"Borrow the Infants' telly and make a pot of tea," suggested Miss Spigot. "Tea-leaf fortunes we could have. Amelia does them a treat! Got a real gift, our Amelia."

"I see us all kneeling," murmured Amelia, stirring the soup with her eyes half closed. "In a big, big room. Flags dangling from the ceiling and purple cushions and a person in a crown saying, "For your services to the kiddies of Pudding Bag School! Rise, Dame Amelia ..."

"Rise, Dame Lacey," murmured Mrs Muldoon, licking a spoon.

"Dame Pansy," sighed Miss Spigot, poking a dumpling.

Then all three of them sighed with delight and smiled in the cabbage-scented air.

After a lot of discussion Class 4b decided to spend the night in their classroom. They moved the chairs and tables to make a space in the middle, piled the dressing-up clothes into a heap on the floor, and lay down on top of it under a layer of coats. Then each of them tried very hard not to think of potato soup and cabbage dumplings. The hot milk flavoured with bicarbonate of soda had been nothing in comparison.

At first it was very cold and draughty, but towards the end of the night it grew

noticeably warmer. The window panes rattled less and less and then stopped. The howl of the wind became a muffled roar and then a gentle murmur.

Madeline Brown woke from a dream of summer and realised that it was morning. The classroom was almost dark but the tops of the windows showed a line of pale light. All around her Class 4b lay sprawled and snoring on piles of old clothes. They looked like leftover jumble from a jumble sale.

There was a distant humming in the air like the sound of the summer bees in her dream.

CHAPTER TWO
Snow up to the Windows

Samantha Freebody was the next person to wake. She rubbed her eyes and stared around the room and tried to remember how she had got there.

"Hello," whispered Madeline.

"Oh!" said Samantha. "Oh Madeline! What did we ...? Why are we ...?"

"Snow," Madeline reminded her.

"Oh yes!"

"Look at the windows!" whispered Madeline.

"Oh," said Samantha, looking. "Oh no! Oh

Madeline! It's right up to the top of them, isn't it?"

"Almost. There's just that little bit left where the light is coming in at the top. I suppose that's why it's so quiet."

"And dark," said Samantha. "Oh Madeline!"

"It will be all right," said Madeline, as bravely as she could.

Snow up to the windows, wrote Simon Percy in his diary, making it official.

On the whole there was very little panic. People were alarmed but also rather excited. Class 4b were used to adventures. After all, they reminded each other, they had faced problems in the past and (helped by some remarkable good luck) overcome them most successfully.

Only the twins were truly frightened. Charlotte and Emma were new that term.

Never in their lives, said Charlotte and Emma, had they had to be with people as alarming as the Pudding Bag School dinner ladies.

"You ought to have seen our old headmaster!" Class 4b told them.

And, continued Charlotte and Emma, never before had they ever spent a single night away from their Mummy and Daddy.

"One night's nothing," said Simon Percy comfortingly. "My parents were away for ten years!"

Charlotte and Emma looked at him in disbelief.

"It's perfectly true," said Dougal McDougal. "They went off in a hot-air balloon and they didn't come back till the end of last term. Not till after we blasted off the rocket."

"What rocket?" asked the twins.

"The rocket we built here at Pudding Bag School to blast our old headmaster into space," said Samuel Moon. "You should have seen it!"

"It was me that launched it," boasted Dougal.

"I was on it!" said Madeline.

"Madeline had to parachute down," Samuel told the twins.

"If you can survive that," said Simon Percy, "you can survive anything! And it's not as if we were stuck here by ourselves. We've got Kate. You're practically grown up, aren't you Kate?"

"Oh, practically," agreed Kate cheerfully as she climbed on to a desk to try and peer through the top of the windows. "What is that funny humming noise?"

The dinner ladies had not been able to get the Infants' television to work, and so they had gone to bed early and spent a cosy night on two armchairs each in front of the open oven door. Morning came as a horrible shock to them.

"It's never gone and snowed all night has it?" demanded Mrs Muldoon.

"I'm afraid it has," said Miss Pilchard.

"Don't tell me we'll be stuck with them kiddies again," said Miss Spigot.

"I'm afraid we will."

The dinner ladies groaned. And then they got out of their armchair beds and did a little investigating and they found that the television still would not work and the phones were dead and the heating was off and the lights were flickering in a worrying kind of way, and worst of all ...

"The kiddies are awake," said Miss Amelia Pilchard.

Strangely, Miss Pilchard's list of bad news brought out the best in Miss Spigot and Mrs Muldoon. They pulled themselves out of their armchairs and began to tackle the problem of breakfast.

"Which is no joke," said Mrs Muldoon. "Seeing as there was no deliveries yesterday, nor will be today and we don't keep in hardly any stores except for the Emergency Freezer."

The Emergency Freezer was where odds and ends of past school dinners were kept.

"But we shall need what's in there for ourselves," said Mrs Muldoon. "We cannot waste it on the kiddies! Make us some toast, Pansy dear, while I have a little think."

Tapioca-and-toast-crust porridge was the result of Mrs Muldoon's little think. The twins almost started weeping again at the sight of it, but Madeline bravely began hers at once.

"That's right!" said Kate. "Come on twins! Close your eyes and get it over with! Scrape your plates everyone! I expect it will only come back hotted up for lunch if you don't!"

Mrs Muldoon came into the dining room a few minutes later to see how they were enjoying their breakfast. She was surprised and pleased to see so many empty plates.

"Eaten the lot!" she announced triumphantly to Miss Spigot and Miss Pilchard.

"And why ever shouldn't they?" demanded Miss Pilchard. "Cocoa everyone? Bananas? I think it's important that we keep up our strength!"

"That's only right," agreed Mrs Muldoon. "If we collapse then where will they be? It's got to be faced. It's us that's in charge."

"And us that will get the blame," added Miss Spigot. "Should anything go wrong."

"Quite true," said Mrs Muldoon. "And that's what I just told the kiddies. Clean plates and no monkey tricks, I said to them! We are well and truly snowed up and the snow ploughs could be Some Time Coming and should we lose anyone through starvation or carelessness then it's us dinner ladies that will cop it!"

"But should we keep the kiddies safe ..." interrupted Miss Pilchard eagerly.

"Through thick and thin," said Miss Spigot.

"Fair means or foul!"

"Against all odds!"

"Then," said Mrs Muldoon, "We will be National Heroines."

"And interviewed on the telly!"

"And Dames, sure as fate!" said Amelia Spigot.

The morning passed very gloomily. The lights were flickering on and off, causing Charlotte and Emma to shiver with misery. Without them the school would be totally dark, the windows by now being completely blotted out with snow.

"It must be because Mr Bedwig's solar panels

are getting snowed up!" exclaimed Madeline suddenly. "You know, he fixed them up last term to run the lights and heat the boiler. That can't be working properly either. No wonder it's got so cold."

"We'll die then," sobbed Charlotte. "We'll freeze in the dark!"

"Of course we won't," said Madeline. "Someone will have to get on to the roof and dig them out, that's all. I don't mind doing it."

"I'll come with you," offered Dougal. "I've got wellies."

"Mrs Muldoon said no monkey tricks," Samantha reminded them. "Don't you think getting on to the roof ..."

"Mrs Muldoon needn't know," interrupted Dougal. "Madeline and I can open the playground door, tunnel up to the surface, scrape off the solar panels and be back before anyone knows we are gone."

That did seem possible. However, when they opened the playground door they had quite a shock. The door opened, as they had expected, on to a solid wall of snow, but it was not normal snow. It creaked. It was as heavy as concrete and as stiff as deep-frozen ice cream. It dented very slightly when kicked but did not crumble.

"You can't tunnel through that," said Simon Percy.

There was a short, gloomy silence during which all the lights went out. It was broken by Madeline who exclaimed triumphantly:

"Look, there's a skylight! Just over our heads! That grey square, in the ceiling. We've only to get through that and we'll be right beside the solar panels! We just need to get some ladders!"

Getting the ladders (which were stored in the basement) in the pitch dark, without attracting the attention of the dinner ladies, was not exactly easy. The trapdoor that led to the basement from under the teacher's desk in Class 4b was a great help though. So was the extreme tidiness of the basement, untouched since the days of Mr Bedwig. Once the ladders had been found, a human chain was formed from trapdoor to cloakroom and they were passed from hand to hand in the darkness.

"Now then!" whispered Kate, when the ladders were finally in place, "Wellies on, Dougal darling! And coat and scarf! And you too, Madeline! I'll hold the ladders steady, Simon and Samuel, you guard the door! If you hear the dinner ladies coming, rush and distract them! Up you go then, Dougal!"

"I've brought Mr Bedwig's broom to help us sweep," Madeline said. "Can you take it, Kate, and pass it up? Oh!"

An avalanche of snow fell into the

cloakroom as Dougal, high above their heads in the darkness, pushed open the skylight. A square of grey sky appeared, blotted out almost straight away by a second avalanche as Dougal heaved himself out.

"What's it like?" called Kate, but Dougal, for once in his life, was lost for words.

Ten metres of snow made an amazing difference to the landscape. All that could be seen of Pudding Bag School was two short, stumpy triangles of roof. Pudding Bag Lane had entirely disappeared. The church tower stuck up from a huge, curving snowdrift. All fences, boundaries, street lights and telephone lines had vanished. All trees were gone, except the most enormous, which were a tangle of the topmost twigs, poking out through the white. To the south there was nothing to be seen but banks of swirling fog, but to the north the multi-storey office blocks of London

rose grey and ghostly in the mist, half their usual height. The humming that Madeline had noticed earlier that morning was now explained. Dozens and dozens of helicopters were disappearing into the north.

"What's it like?" called Kate again.

"Fantastic!" shouted Dougal.

"Can you walk on it safely?"

"Yes, yes, it's frozen solid!"

"Get on with it then, Dougal darling," said Kate. "It's awfully dark down here. Madeline's on her way to help you. Are you all right, Madeline?"

"Quite all right," called Madeline, pulling herself on to the roof and making her way towards the nearest solar panel. They were easy to find, a double line of them, drifted up in sweeping curves, only just beneath the level of the snow.

Madeline began to sweep and Dougal

scooped and scraped with his hands and before long a faint cheer from below told them that the lights were back on.

"Come down now!" called Kate. "Simon says the dinner ladies are beginning to lay the tables for lunch. They'll be looking for us any moment."

"All right!" called Dougal, and a minute later he and Madeline were back down the ladder again.

"Whatever is that enormous smell of fish?" asked Madeline.

"Lunch," said Kate. "Courage everyone!"

Lunch however, was not too bad at all and the dinner ladies cheered by the miraculous return of electricity, sang as they served.

Lavender's blue, diddle diddle,
Lavender's green.
When you are King, diddle diddle …

Here they broke off giggling, because Queen was too much to hope for, even Amelia couldn't quite imagine that. Presently, however, they found new words.

> *Lavender's blue, diddle diddle*
> *Vi'lets the same.*
> *When we escape, diddle diddle,*
> *I'll be a …*

Class 4b could not quite make out the last word, it was lost in gales of laughter. Nor could they decide exactly what was in the fish cakes.

"Tapioca of course," said Kate, who had already realised that tapioca went into nearly everything the dinner ladies cooked. "But there's something else that makes them that lovely shade of pink."

Whatever it was, it was, and second helpings were accepted very cheerfully. Only Madeline and Bagdemagus seemed not to be happy. Madeline was busy thinking of the dozens of helicopters she had seen disappearing over the horizon and she did not notice what she ate. Nobody knew what was the matter with Bagdemagus. He prowled round the table, spitting and swearing and arching in fury whenever a dinner lady passed.

Pudding was plain tapioca but everyone was too full up to mind.

After lunch the dinner ladies withdrew to the kitchen to celebrate their success with hot chocolate and oven chips and afternoon naps. As soon as they were safely out of the way Class 4b divided into two groups. The more intrepid (led by Dougal McDougal) spent an exciting afternoon tobogganing on the school roof. The others began a careful search for somewhere to sleep that night.

"We must find somewhere better than that classroom floor," said Kate. "Just in case we are not rescued today."

"Somewhere without windows," said Samantha. The ghostly reflections of Class 4b in the snowed-up classroom windows had frightened her very much the night before. It was Madeline who thought of Mr Bedwig's basement, and as soon as she suggested it everyone realised that it was the perfect place. It was warm, heated by the solar-powered boiler, and draught free, and had no blank, snow-blotted windows. Also it had a friendly feel about it, a sort of echo of Mr Bedwig himself, always reassuring and cheerful and matter-of-fact.

"It's just like he's only this minute gone

away," said Simon. "I wonder if he's worrying about us."

"Mummy will be worrying," remarked Charlotte dolefully, "and Daddy! Daddy will be frantic, won't he, Emma?"

"Think how pleased they'll be when they discover you're perfectly safe," said Kate comfortingly. "What's that you've found Madeline?"

It was a small transistor radio. They switched it on at once, and very soon afterwards they discovered that no one was worrying about them at all.

"... The successful evacuation of blizzard-bound London," came a newsreader's voice "... is now considered complete. The entire population helicopter-lifted to safety ..."

"That's what those helicopters were doing!" exclaimed Madeline.

"... The retreat to the sun-soaked North!"

continued the news report between bursts of static "... a triumph of planning ... not a single casualty, complaint or missing person report has been received!"

"What about us?" squeaked Samantha indignantly.

"... Temporary schools are all ready open ..."

"Listen! Listen!" said Kate.

"... in empty Scottish castles ... hospitals all moved to the invigorating air of low season holiday camps ..."

The voice was getting fainter and fainter, as if the speaker was drifting further and further away.

"... Prime Minister congratulated ... no cause for alarm ... contact numbers for families to be announced in the next few days ..."

The sound was growing fainter and fainter.

"The batteries must be nearly flat," said Madeline.

"... now over to the weather forecast ..."

But to everyone's great disappointment the sound faded completely before the weather forecast could begin.

"Blinkin' 'eck!" said Mrs Muldoon, peering out through a crack of open kitchen door when Kate went to tell her the news. "Everyone's gone, did you say?"

"I'm afraid so."

"Parked the schools in empty castles, have they?"

"That's what we heard."

"Not noticed they haven't got us then?"

"They don't seem to have."

"Pity you didn't hear the weather forecast! It's thundering at the moment, by the sound of it!"

"Wrong, Lacey dear!"

Amelia Pilchard had appeared suddenly in the corridor behind Kate.

"Wrong, wrong, wrong! Lacey dear," she repeated. "That's not thunder. That's Something On The Roof and Pansy and I know what!"

"Kiddies!" said Miss Spigot, popping up behind her. "That brother of Young Kate's here, and his gang! Up there with tea trays – sledging!"

"Never!" exclaimed Mrs Muldoon.

"Got a ladder in the cloakroom," continued Miss Spigot. "We slipped up a moment ago and caught them red handed!"

"Oh, I'm sure they didn't mean any harm!" exclaimed Kate, but it was no use. That was the end of the tobogganing on the roof. Mrs Muldoon, already upset by the radio news, was very angry indeed. She did not wish, she said, to be held responsible for young persons hurling themselves to their deaths, and Miss Spigot and Miss Pilchard completely agreed.

Class 4b were told that they were in disgrace. There was no repeat of the lunchtime concert of "Lavender's Blue" that evening. At suppertime plates of bubble and squeak and rabbit stew were handed round with such grim expressions that nobody dared to say a word until the dinner ladies were safely back in the kitchen.

"They do like to keep that kitchen door tight shut," remarked Samuel Moon.

"They think that way they'll keep us from knowing what we're eating," said Dougal. "They won't though! Right then! Potato and that cabbage again, that's the bubble and squeak. Can anyone work out what's in this stew?"

"Beetroot, tapioca," said Madeline, sorting carefully with her fork, "and the brown stuff

must be rabbit I suppose. I didn't know rabbit was so nasty. I've never had it before."

"Grrrrr!" said Bagdemagus, glaring at Madeline's forkful of rabbit stew.

Bagdemagus knows something that we do not, wrote Simon Percy in his diary after supper that night. *I wonder what it is.*

CHAPTER THREE
What Bagdemagus Knew

By night time the camp in the basement was complete. Miss Pilchard (prowling the empty classrooms for her own private purposes) had inspected it and said it gave her the cold horrors. Mrs Muldoon and Miss Spigot (walking off their late supper of chicken nuggets and poptarts) said it put them in mind of an open grave, but Class 4b loved it.

It was wonderfully homely. Sledging clothes steamed cosily on the hot-water pipes and boots and shoes dried on the boiler. The games cupboard had been emptied and the sleeping arrangements (constructed on two levels so as to save floor space) were now in place. Hammocks had been made by hanging football and cricket nets from the floor joists of the classrooms above. Beneath them several thicknesses of PE mats set out in a row made a long, continual mattress. There were no arguments about who should sleep where. At bedtime the more reckless people (led by Dougal McDougal) grabbed the hammocks, while the more prudent (led by Madeline Brown) chose the PE mats underneath. When everybody was in place for the night Kate covered them up with the two ancient red velvet curtains that had once hung over the Pudding Bag School stage.

Then Bagdemagus curled up on Madeline's chest and Kate tucked herself up at the end of the mattress bed and Samuel Moon surprised them all by sitting up and reading aloud from

a book of Antarctic exploration that he had discovered in the school library. It told of dripping snow caves and frozen sleeping bags, feasts of raw penguin and seal-liver stew, weeks of darkness when the sun never rose above the horizon, journeys so bitter that the sledge runners froze to the ground, ice-covered seas and howling blizzards. Listening as Samuel's solemn, husky voice described such awfulnesses was very comforting. Even Charlotte and Emma began to think that things might be very much worse. The boiler purred like a cat and the red velvet curtains felt very cosy.

One by one Class 4b snuggled down and fell asleep.

Bagdemagus did not purr. He spent a restless night and woke Madeline very early by trampling on her stomach. He waited

impatiently as she crawled out of bed and, as
soon as she was properly up, seized her by the
toe of a sock and tried to drag her out of the
basement.

"Hi! Stop it! Wait till I get my shoes on!"
said Madeline.

Bagdemagus sat down and growled while
Madeline tied her laces and then led her at a
great rate out of the basement, along grey,
empty corridors, and at last to the kitchen door.

"Do you want to go in?" asked Madeline, very puzzled.

Bagdemagus shook his head.

"What then?"

Bagdemagus began to prance. He pranced and patted and jumped and sprang at the large and smelly dustbin that had been parked outside the kitchen door by the dinner ladies the night before.

"Oh, that!" said Madeline, and was about to lift the lid when Mrs Muldoon appeared, bustling suddenly from the kitchen with a pile of plates and a seething saucepan.

"Now then young lady," said Mrs Muldoon. "No call for you to be a-poking and a-prying round here!"

"I wasn't," said Madeline. "Only Bagdemagus seemed to want to show me this dustbin. Is it here for anything special?"

"It is where it is," said Mrs Muldoon with

dignity, hurrying Madeline into the dining room, "because my assistants and I did not wish to sleep with it. Miss Nosy Parker! Spoons, Amelia dear!"

"Coming!" called Miss Pilchard, and a moment later came in with a handful of spoons, each of which she polished with a fog of breath and a rub with a small furry rag before arranging them daintily around the table.

"No children here but this one?" she enquired between huffs.

"None but her," agreed Mrs Muldoon. "Pansy still busy?"

"Topping and tailing," said Miss Pilchard. "Fiddly, she says."

"This one's been enquiring about the bin," Mrs Muldoon informed her.

Amelia Pilchard darted a very cold look at Madeline as she laid down the last of the spoons but before she could speak Class 4b arrived, clattering into the dining hall. Under cover of the noise Madeline slipped out of the room for a moment, lifted the lid of the dustbin and peered swiftly inside.

"It was absolutely full of cat-food tins," she told her classmates later on, when breakfast (tapioca and potato porridge) had been consumed and they were crowded together in one of the cloakrooms, washing faces and tidying hair and cleaning teeth with fingers dipped in dining-room salt (Kate's idea).

"Perhaps he was trying to tell you he was hungry," suggested Simon.

"Perhaps," agreed Madeline uncertainly. "But if he's eaten all those tins I don't see how he could be. Oh! Oh Simon! I've just remembered something awful! The classroom pets! All this time we've been snowed up here and nobody has fed the classroom pets!"

That shocked everyone. Bagdemagus and his problems were forgotten as Class 4b hurried to the rescue. The Infants' gerbil collection had been forgotten for nearly two days. So had Class 4a's stick insects, the office goldfish, the Class 2 guinea pig family, Ant Planet, and the pedigree black-and-white mice.

"There aren't half as many gerbils as there used to be," remarked Simon Percy, as he filled up their feeding bowls. "When I was an Infant there seemed to be hundreds! Same with the stick insects."

"There still are an awful lot of stick insects," remarked Samantha with a shudder. "Don't look at me like that Madeline! I can bear being brave about being snowed up and eating the dinner ladies' cooking and sleeping in the basement and nobody knowing we are here, but I can't be brave about stick insects!"

"Neither can I really," agreed Madeline. "I pretend I don't mind them, but secretly I do. I was wondering if we ought to take all the pets down to the basement with us?"

"What all those mice and Bagdemagus?" asked Dougal, laughing. "I don't think so!"

"You're probably right," agreed Madeline, looking worriedly at Bagdemagus as she spoke.

He was still in a terrible temper.

"He has gone thin!" said Simon suddenly.

"Bagdemagus has?"

"Yes, look at him! He used to look so bouncy and he doesn't anymore. He looks like he's going down, like an old balloon."

Madeline bent down and burrowed her fingers into Bagdemagus's thick, marmalade coat and found that Simon was quite right. Underneath his fur he was quite bony. She thought of the empty cat-food tins and she thought of Bagdemagus, growling with temper around the dustbin and she was struck by a horrible idea. And then she pushed the idea to the back of her mind and hurried off to the kitchen where the cat food was kept to beg an early lunch for Bagdemagus.

Amelia Pilchard opened the door and very unwillingly handed over a half-filled tin of Whiskas, which Bagdemagus devoured in three starving gulps.

"I think he'd like some more," said Madeline.

"There is no more," said Miss Pilchard briefly, and Madeline pushed her horrible idea even further to the back of her mind. Instead she enquired about the strange, earthy, fusty, smell that was escaping from the kitchen.

"Nut roast," Amelia Pilchard told her. "Now off with you both!"

Madeline, returning through the entrance

hall, was not very surprised to notice that the displays entitled "Our Autumn Harvest" that had decorated its walls for weeks, had mysteriously disappeared.

The nut roast was served with Crispy Pancake Rolls and Dougal McDougal found something very strange in his.

"It's a hairclip," he said, spitting it out and inspecting it.

"It's not," said Kate, peering over to look.

"One of those things for scraping out your nails then!"

"Don't be revolting, Dougal darling! Anyway, it's not one of those. What's it made of?"

"Plastic I think."

"I've seen something like it before," said Kate. "It must be a part of one of those little toys they give away in cereal packets. It's got mixed up with the cooking somehow. Throw

it away Dougal darling! Thank goodness you
didn't choke!"

Dougal put it in his pocket and forgot
about it.

"Forty-eight hours, Dames Pansy and
Pilchard!" said Mrs Muldoon, in the kitchen
that afternoon. "Forty-eight hours and not a
soul have we lost nor a meal have they missed!
Pansy dear, are you starting supper already?
What did you decide should be done with the
you-know-what's that were so fiddly to top
and tail?"

"Kebabs," replied Miss Spigot, ramming
bundles on long pointed sticks as she spoke.
"I'm kebabing them! It is a well-known fact,
Dame Lacey, that kiddies will eat anything
that is stuck on a stick! Amelia is doing a nice
tapioca shape, coloured with the last of the
beetroot for pudding. Should you say three

damehoods were in the bag, Lacey dear?"

Mrs Muldoon said that she did not doubt it at all and Amelia Pilchard closed her eyes and in a visionary trance saw them all in a National Tribute on Prime-Time TV. She described it so well that very soon Mrs Muldoon and Miss Spigot saw it too. It was all very pleasant and flattering (though no more than they deserved) and they were all three of them in a very good temper when Kate knocked on the door. Kate asked if it would be all right if she went up on to the roof to see if there were any signs of help arriving.

"After all," remarked Mrs Muldoon, when Kate had been given their gracious approval and gone off to fetch the ladder. "Somebody's got to, I suppose, and if push comes to shove it's not as if she is one of ours!" Which meant, as the other two dinner ladies completely understood, that if Kate fell to her death or was lost in the snow or anything else of that kind then they could not possibly be held responsible.

Kate, standing on the ladder with her head and shoulders out of the skylight, was astonished to see sunshine and blue sky. No snow had fallen since the night before. The tracks of the roof-tobogganing party were as clear and sharp as if they had just been made. She reached out to touch a blue-shadowed footprint and found that the snow was as hard as ice. There was no sign of life in any direction, not a sound, or a movement, or a bird in the sky. Nor was there anything, Kate realised, that would show any passing helicopter that a class full of children and three dinner ladies were stranded deep beneath the snow.

We should make a sign, thought Kate.

Something that someone could see flying over.

"I need something black," she called down the ladder to Class 4b, waiting below. "Something black that will show up on the snow and make a mark for the rescue helicopters to see."

"Are there rescue helicopters?" asked Charlotte hopefully.

"Bound to be dozens sooner or later," said Kate as cheerfully as she could, considering the emptiness of the sky. "Now what can we use? Soot would do."

"What about black powder paint?" asked Emma and was very pleased when Kate said at once that powder paint would be perfect.

Several people ran off to hunt for some straight away and half-a-dozen tins were collected and handed up the ladder. Soon Kate was out on the roof, marking a large but rather wobbly cross over the lumps and bumps of the surrounding snowdrifts.

"There!" she said, triumphantly. "Anyone could see that for miles! And if it snows more I will just go out and do it again."

"Until someone comes?" asked Charlotte.

"That's right," said Kate hopefully. "Until someone comes."

The tapioca shape, coloured with the last of the beetroot was horrible, but the kebabs were utterly delicious. Only Madeline did not enjoy them. She gave hers to Bagdemagus who swished his tail with pleasure.

"What's the matter, Madeline?" asked Charlotte from across the table.

"Nothing," said Madeline untruthfully, and was very glad that Bagdemagus could not talk.

Bagdemagus could not talk, but other people besides Madeline could work things out.

Dougal McDougal was the next one to understand what was happening at Pudding Bag School mealtimes. He fell out of his hammock in the middle of the night, landing on top of Madeline, and bringing Simon Percy down with him.

"I dreamed about my pancake roll," he began, even before he had picked himself up. "I dreamed about my pancake roll and I ..."

"Shush! Shush!" whispered Madeline. "You'll wake everyone up!"

"... dreamed about that thing I found in it, and I suddenly knew ..."

"Stop talking so loudly!" begged Madeline. "Come up to the classroom! Simon, come on! Take his other arm! Make him come out of the basement before he gets everyone up!"

"Why?" asked Simon, still dopey with sleep. "What's all the fuss about? What's the matter with Dougal? What's going on?"

"No wonder they were crispy!" hissed Dougal, as he followed Simon and Madeline up the stepladder that led into their classroom. "A stick insect's leg! That's what it was! No wonder Kate thought she'd seen one before! She'd just been helping to feed them. And I don't see why we're being so careful to be quiet about it, Madeline Brown!"

Madeline carefully closed the trapdoor and sat on it before replying.

"Imagine the twins if they knew they'd eaten Crispy Stick Insect Pancake Rolls!"

"Crispy Stick Insect Pancake Rolls!" repeated Simon Percy in horror.

"Yes, or cat-food fish cakes!"

"Cat-food fish cakes!"

"Prime Cut Salmon Whiskas we ate, and Rabbit Chunks with Savoury Jelly!"

Simon and Dougal stared at her, speechless and green.

"It's true! I saw the tins in the dustbin. Bagdemagus showed me. He knew."

"When did you know?" demanded Dougal accusingly.

"I only really believed at suppertime. When I saw those kebabs ..."

"What!"

"And remembered what Simon said about the gerbils. How there used to be thousands ..."

"I'm going to wake everyone up and tell them right now!" said Dougal.

"You mustn't," said Madeline. "It would just

make them sick, and what's the point of that? And people like Charlotte and Emma will be really frightened. And after all, I suppose it's better than actually starving ..."

Simon and Dougal looked at her in amazement.

"Actually starving," repeated Dougal slowly, and he looked round at the bleak, snow-buried windows and the empty classroom.

The date on the blackboard was now three days old. The tulips on Miss Gilhoolie's desk had dropped their petals and died. It all seemed suddenly to be very bleak and lonely, but just then Bagdemagus appeared from the shadows, climbed on to Dougal's lap, and began to purr.

After all, Bagdemagus eats cat food, Simon wrote bravely in his diary the next morning. *And he's all right.*

CHAPTER FOUR
Something Else to Cook

We must find the dinner ladies something else to cook," announced Madeline the next morning. After a breakfast of fried beetroot that did not seem unreasonable to anyone. So the great food hunt began.

Simon Percy recorded the results in his diary.

From the Cloakrooms
7 half-packets of crisps (rubbish bins)
4 very old apples (one bitten)
1 banana and 1/2 packet of Rolos (under radiator)

1 packet of baby rusks (some missing) from Infant's shoe bag

From Class 4a's Kitchen Art Exhibition
2 carrots, 2 onions, 1 leek and 1/2 a pickled cabbage

From the lockers
27 packets of sweets with one left in the bottom
1 Cornish pasty (given to Bagdemagus)

From the teachers' desks
122 packets of confiscated chewing gum
1 box of Mr Kipling Fondant Fancies (2 missing)

Also
1 packet mustard and cress seed
14 bean bags (PE cupboard)

The sweets were shared out and eaten immediately. Charlotte and Emma were

handed the mustard and cress to plant, which
they did with a mixture of awful pride (at
being given such an important responsibility)
and awful fear (at the thought of still being
snowed up when it was ready to harvest).
The baby rusks were put aside for a direr
emergency ("Direr than this," said Kate).

"What about the rest?" asked Emma.

"The rest will have to be given to the dinner
ladies," said Kate.

The dinner ladies had their own private list of
food supplies pinned up on the kitchen wall.
It was worryingly short (and alarmingly alive).
It was:

Tapioca (very little left)

14 gerbils

3 fish

4 guinea pigs

12 black-and-white mice

That Cat

"I don't know what we'd do with the cat!" said Mrs Muldoon, looking at the list. "It would have to be curry, unless we did soup. And after that we will be down to Rock Bottom and you know what that means!"

Miss Pilchard and Miss Spigot knew very well what it meant. Rock Bottom was the supply of odds and ends of school-dinner food in the Emergency Freezer that they were keeping for their own private enjoyment.

"Not that it is anything like the Good Home Cooking the kiddies are getting," Miss Spigot often remarked as she rooted round for Dino Burgers or Instant Trifle or whatever was on the menu for the dinner ladies that day. All three dinner ladies were very relieved when Kate and Madeline turned up with the new supplies. Over the next three days they were recycled into:

Mixed Fruit Pudding
Bean and Vegetable Curry
Bean Hot Pot
Vegetable Bake with Crispy Topping
Bean Surprise (twice)

During this time a lot more snow fell. The solar panels had to be cleared again and again. It was usually Kate who went up on to the roof to do this job, and each time she found it more and more difficult and depressing. There was never any sign of rescue. She would have given up bothering to mark the powder paint cross on the snow altogether if the twins had not constantly reminded her. Charlotte and Emma had cheered up a lot over the last few days, especially since their mustard and cress had begun to sprout.

Simon Percy kept a careful account of the meals produced by the dinner ladies on the days following the food hunt, and ticked them off against the list of supplies in his diary as they went along. Therefore it was a great shock to him when, on the evening of the third day, supper was not Mr Kipling Fondant Fancies and Chewing Gum (as he had confidently expected) but Golden Tapioca Fish Fingers instead.

Most of Class 4b ate their fish fingers without a second thought but Simon pushed his away, and Madeline offered hers to Bagdemagus, who ate it with melancholy, downcast eyes. She caught Simon's glance as he watched and gave a tiny nod of understanding.

"The office goldfish," their eyes told each other and each of them wondered silently,

What on earth is going to be next?

That night when they were all in bed Samuel
Moon described to them a rescue that he had
read about in his Antarctic explorers book.

"They were marooned," he said. "On a little
stony island. Their ship had sunk and they had
eaten nearly all the food …"

"There's still our mustard and cress,"
whispered Charlotte to Emma. "Growing all
the time!"

"… And nobody came to rescue them,"
went on Samuel. "Nobody could because
nobody knew they were there …"

Madeline gave a little sigh.

"And it was terrible weather of course."

"So what did they do?" interrupted Dougal.
"Die?"

"Shut up, Dougal darling," said Kate briskly.
"Of course they didn't die! None of them died,

did they, Samuel?"

"No," said Samuel. "None of them died. They had a few supplies left, just enough for a rescue party to set out with ..."

"Oh, oh!" began Emma and Charlotte excitedly, both struck with the same brilliant idea at once. "Oh, we've thought of something! Go on, Samuel!"

"So a few of them packed up and left the others. They travelled north. They sailed away in an open boat ..."

"We haven't got an open boat," said Charlotte and Emma, very disappointed all of a sudden.

"And did they find help?" asked Madeline.

"Yes."

"And they got back in time to rescue their friends?"

"Yes, yes!"

"Before they had to eat the cat?"

"What are you talking about?"

"I didn't mean to say that," said Madeline hastily. "I got muddled up. But that's what we are going to have to do, isn't it? We will have to go and look for help. And we will travel north like they did, because that's where the radio said everyone had gone to ..."

"The dinner ladies will never let you," said Samantha.

"We'll go without telling them."

"How will you get out? They keep the ladder in the kitchen and all the doors are blocked with tons and tons of snow."

"We'll dig a tunnel. Don't you remember when Mr Bedwig was here? How he made us an escape passage so that we could get out of school without Mr Jones knowing? It went through the place in the basement where the coal used to come in."

"But, Madeline," protested Kate at this

85

point. "How could anyone possibly manage? They might have to go miles and miles before they found anyone. It would be much too dangerous?"

"It's the only thing to do," said Madeline.

That reminded Class 4b of the time when Madeline had decided the only thing to do was to blast their terrible headmaster into deepest space. Madeline was usually so quiet that it was hard to believe that she had such astonishing ideas, but she had been quite right then, and probably she was quite right now.

"We will need a tent or something like that to sleep in," she said.

"Madeline!" said Kate. "It's not camping weather!"

"Actually," said Samuel earnestly. "They camped out in the Antarctic in much worse weather than this. And a tent would be much quicker than having to build an igloo at the end of each day."

"And we would need sleeping bags,"
continued Madeline, " and emergency
supplies ..."

"It is very important not to get scurvy," said
Samuel. "You will need plenty of vegetables."

"Mustard and cress is vegetables," said
Emma.

"Just the thing!" said Madeline. "And we
would need a sledge to carry everything on!"

"How would you know which way to go?"
asked Samantha.

"Easy in the daytime," said Madeline.
"North is where the tower blocks are thickest.
I expect you can still see them sticking up,
can't you Kate?"

"Bits of them," said Kate dubiously.

"And there will be stars at night."

"Not if it's snowing," pointed out Kate. "And
it's been foggy a lot lately too."

"Well, we'll take Bagdemagus," said Madeline, suddenly inspired. "Cats always know their way home, everyone knows that! We'll take Bagdemagus and which ever way he points we'll go in the opposite direction! As long as we start off going north he will always point south. He can be a compass cat!"

"Who'll go?" asked Samantha, and there was silence.

Earlier that afternoon Kate had found a candle in an ancient cardboard box. It was made of beeswax.

"I remember that candle," Simon Percy had remarked when he saw it. "It's from when we did our Bee Project, ages ago, when we were Infants. We went to a farm and saw honey being made."

"On a boiling hot day," said Dougal, joining in. "You couldn't eat the ice cream fast enough to stop it melting."

"It was proper countryside," said Samuel Moon dreamily.

"We had a picnic in a field that was all covered in buttercups," said Madeline. "And when you lay down and looked up it was like they whirled above your head like planets. And Simon said, "Why does the ground hum?" And the farmer said, 'Because it's alive.' "

"I remember," said Simon.

"And we brought back honey fudge and pencils with bees on their tops and a real honeycomb and that candle."

Now the candle was alight, filling the basement with the hot sweet scent of summer. It was very quiet and still. Only Bagdemagus was restless, his prowling shadow moving among shadows on the wall. Shadows of hammocks, shadow boots and shadow books and shadow heads hung in thought.

"I'll go," said Charlotte. "If somebody will come with me."

"I will," said Emma at once. "And there'll be Madeline, won't there Madeline?"

Madeline nodded while the rest of Class 4b stared at the twins. That candle-lit memory of summer had been too much for most of them. It was one thing to plan a winter journey across a deserted, snow-buried city, but it was quite another to say you would actually go. Even Madeline, who had known from the start that she would not escape, shivered at the thought.

Now she said, "I don't think both twins ought to go."

"I don't think anyone ought to go," said Kate. "Don't look at me like that Dougal darling! And don't say what I think you're going to say!"

"Well I'm getting sick of being stuck indoors," said Dougal. "Anyway it might be quite fun."

"It couldn't be any worse than the Antarctic was," agreed Samuel. "I don't mind going."

"Good," said Dougal. "That should be enough then. Bagdemagus, he's got to because he's the compass cat and anyway he'll be safer with us. Sam. He's the Antarctic expert. Me. I'm not being left out. Madeline because she thought of it, and one of the twins but not both in case we don't make it! No good you sticking your hand up like that, Simon! You get asthma, you know you do! And don't bother saying you'll come, Kate, because they'll need you here. Somebody's got to keep the solar panels clear. I think we ought to start getting ready tonight! Simon might be right, and it might be Fondant Fancies and chewing gum for breakfast, but if he's wrong, there's no time to waste!"

"Shut up Dougal!" exclaimed Madeline and Simon because the sad fate of the stick insects, gerbils and goldfish was still a secret from most of the class.

"No," said Dougal. "I won't shut up! We ought to tell if they are going to be left behind with the dinner ladies."

It was too late after that to stop. That is how Class 4b learnt that they had already eaten the cat food, the office goldfish, most of the gerbils and about half the stick insects. Also that the supplies they had discovered on the great food hunt were almost gone, and that it was only a matter of time until ...

Here Bagdemagus laid back his ears and yowled.

"Poor Bagdemagus, you shan't be cooked," promised Samantha, and with that everyone jumped out of bed and the preparations for the

Relief Expedition North began at once.

Icy-cold and musty-smelling air filled the basement as Mr Bedwig's escape passage was opened up for the first time that term. To everyone's delight the Christmas lights, which were strung along its winding length, were found to be still working. The passage ended in steps and a double trapdoor that, in normal weather, opened out on to Pudding Bag Lane. Now, of course, it opened out on to snow.

"You'll never get through that," said Kate thankfully. "It's solid ice."

"We will," said Madeline. "We'll have to. Don't you see that we'll have to, Kate?"

"Of course she does," said Dougal.

After the escape passage had been opened up and inspected, people turned to searching through the basement cupboards for anything that might possibly be of any use.

"If only we could find something else for the dinner ladies to cook," said Samantha, looking at Bagdemagus, and a few minutes later she made a wonderful discovery. A huge pile of beanbags, bursting at the seams and put aside for repair, but still, as Samantha said joyfully, perfectly edible.

"Well done Samantha!" said Kate, "And look what I've found! Nearly a whole sack-full too!"

"What is it?" demanded a circle of excited people.

"Grass seed!"

"What's grass seed doing down here?"

"Mr Bedwig put grass seed over the bonfire site where we launched the rocket from," remembered Simon Percy. "It must be left over from that."

"But can you eat grass seed?"

"Oh yes," said Simon at once. "My parents lived on stuff like that when their hot-air balloon crashed in the Himalayan foothills. Especially before they tamed the yaks."

"That's all right then," said Samantha, sighing with relief.

"Yes," said Kate. "Now they won't have to go."

But the members of the relief expedition said at once that this was not true. It was either a case of going now, they said, leaving everyone behind eating grass seed and beanbags, or going in three or four days time, when the grass seed and beanbags had run out, leaving everyone behind ...

"But we might be rescued any day," said Kate.

"If you are," said Madeline, "you can come and look for us. But I don't think we will be. I don't think anyone even knows we are here. I think our families just think we are living in some remote Scottish castle not bothering to write."

Kate stopped arguing after that and told herself that anyway no one could go anywhere until a tunnel had been dug, not to mention a sledge and tent and sleeping bags conjured up from nowhere. She took herself to bed, hoping everyone else would follow her example, but all around her the preparations for the relief expedition went on far into the night.

CHAPTER FIVE
Beanbags and Grass Seed

Samuel Moon had the sort of watch that could be programmed to ring an alarm.

"Thank goodness!" said Class 4b, who had decided that the sooner the grass seed and beanbags were delivered to the dinner ladies the next morning, the better it would be. Breakfast might, as some people still tried to hope, be Fondant Fancies and chewing gum, but on the other hand it might not. Class 4b thought of the guinea pigs and remaining gerbils and black-and-white mice and set Samuel's alarm for five o'clock in the morning.

Five minutes after it went off he and Dougal and Simon Percy had arrived at the kitchen door.

"I expect they're still asleep in there," said Dougal. "Better bash really hard if we want to wake them up! Stand back and I'll ... Oh!"

Even before he had raised his hand, the kitchen door began to open. For a moment, seeing the grey emptiness that lay behind, they thought it had done it of its own accord, but then into the nothingness Miss Pilchard appeared. She wore a large plastic apron and pink rubber gloves, and clasped a very big pair of kitchen scissors.

"What a delicious surprise!" she remarked, showing no surprise at all, and she snipped with her scissors at the air in front of her. The blades made a lively, scrunching sound as they opened and shut.

"Crikey, Miss Pilchard!" exclaimed Dougal

McDougal. "Crikey, Miss Pilchard! You do look … er … you do look …"

Dougal's voice trailed into silence. Miss Pilchard was looking down at the three of them with a sort of cold, thinking curiosity, as if planning how she would pad them out, should it ever come to cooking in the end. It was so frightening a look that Samuel could not stand it. He dumped his beanbags and fled back to the basement.

Simon would have liked very much to follow Samuel, but Miss Pilchard's gaze was now concentrated upon Dougal and himself. Dougal seemed to be still completely stunned and was no help at all, so it was Simon who ended up explaining, "We found this stuff in one of the basement cupboards, Miss Pilchard. We thought it would do for cooking."

Snack, snack! went the scissors blades, one final time.

"More or less anything will do for cooking," remarked Miss Pilchard, smiling at her scissors.

"There's loads of beanbags," Simon told her. "And all this grass seed which we thought ... Oh, Mrs Muldoon!"

Mrs Muldoon, shoeless and rumpled and puffy with sleep, had never looked so beautiful as she did to Simon and Dougal at that moment. Everything suddenly became normal again. Dougal came out of his trance, and Simon eagerly explained, "We were just showing Miss Pilchard the things we found last night!"

"Food!" said Dougal.

"Grass seed," said Miss Pilchard, looking at Dougal with dislike. "Grass seed, Mrs Muldoon, and more of those beans. It seems we will have to devise a vegetarian menu for today, after all!"

Dougal and Simon glanced at each other and longed to speak.

"Grass seed and beans are all very well," said Mrs Muldoon. "Not what one would wish perhaps, but I daresay we will manage something. But if you were to ask me, Miss Pilchard," she continued, glaring at Dougal. "I would say grass seed and beans was not the half of it! Guilty as guilty, these two look! What have you been up to, out of bed so early? Messing about on that roof?"

"No, no!" Dougal and Simon assured her at once.

"I won't have you poking through the dustbins. I told that Madeline so the other day!"

"We haven't been doing! We haven't done anything like that!"

"No quarrelling or breaking your necks with silly games?"

"No, Mrs Muldoon!"

"I am pleased to hear it," said Mrs Muldoon. "I shouldn't like to ask Miss Spigot to spend her nights in that basement with you! I shouldn't like to, and I couldn't stick it myself, having a nervous fear of being buried alive. And neither could Miss Pilchard, so highly strung as she is. But only last night Miss Spigot said to me, 'I can and I will, Mrs Muldoon, for the sake of the kiddies! If you ask me to I will!' "

Dougal and Simon looked at each other in unconcealed horror.

"So I give you fair warning," said Mrs Muldoon triumphantly. "Any monkey business and down she will be and there she will stay until rescue arrives. "No sacrifice is too great," she said to me last night. "No sacrifice is too great, Mrs Muldoon, for the sake of those blessed kiddies!" She is a woman in a million and Miss Pilchard here is another, if you did but know it ..."

Miss Pilchard bowed her head and closed her eyes and Mrs Muldoon turned aside to mop away invisible tears. Dougal and Simon prudently seized the moment and bolted.

"That's give them something to think about!" commented Mrs Muldoon briskly as she put her handkerchief away, and she and Miss Pilchard laughed very loudly together.

Meanwhile Samuel Moon had returned to the basement in a state of panic.

"We were only just in time!" he told Class 4b. "She had rubber gloves and a plastic apron and great snapping scissors, all ready for goodness knows what! I bet it would have been guinea pig for breakfast if we hadn't arrived when we did! I think everybody should get out of bed at once, and dig for their lives!"

"Dig what?" demanded Kate, yawning and yawning, only half awake.

"The escape tunnel! So that the relief expedition can go for help straight away. She's dead weird, that Miss Pilchard, you ask Dougal and Simon!"

Samuel's alarm was catching and when Simon and Dougal returned a few minutes later they agreed that he was quite right. Work began almost at once, organised by Madeline Brown, who had invented a method of ice-tunnel digging in the middle of the night.

She soon had everyone organised. One team of people hacked at the ice face with whatever they could find, hammers and screw drivers from the school toolbox, cricket bats, unused rocket parts and the long handled shovel that had been used to stoke the boiler in the days before solar power took over. A second team piled the excavated snow and ice into waste-paper bins. A third emptied the bins into the basement sink and ran the hot

tap over them until the ice was melted.

"That's the best job," said Madeline. "We had better take turns at it so that everyone gets a chance to warm their hands up!"

Mr Bedwig's escape passage had been the old entrance by which coal was delivered to Pudding Bag School. A wooden trapdoor in the middle of Pudding Bag Lane had led down a long chute to the boiler room. Mr Bedwig had cleaned it out, painted it white and added Christmas tree lights and steps. Madeline's excavation system worked so efficiently that by eight o'clock that morning the worst of the work was already done. The tunnel through the snow was as long again as the escape passage, sloping steeply upwards and carved along one edge in the form of rough steps.

"I wish I could think of something that we could use for a tent," Madeline said to Simon as they returned together from the ice face for a hand-warming session at the basement sink. "I think we are going to need one. I read in Samuel's book that an expert eskimo with the right kind of snow could construct an igloo in fifteen to twenty-five minutes, but how do we know we are going to find the right kind of snow?"

"Or an expert eskimo," added Dougal, who was also warming his hands.

Madeline laughed but then looked serious again as she stirred the lumps of ice melting in the sink.

"It needs to be the sort you can cut into blocks, but Kate says the snow on the roof is as soft as soft, too powdery even for snowballs, and this stuff from underneath is solid ice."

"You'll think of something," said Simon comfortingly. "You always do! I wonder how the dinner ladies are getting on with the beanbags and grass seed. I'm starving to death!"

Madeline volunteered to go up and see, and also to feed and count the classroom pets. She returned a few minutes later to say that breakfast was ready and that the gerbils and guinea pigs were all present and correct.

"What about the black-and-white mice?" asked several people. Madeline said nothing, but looked reproachfully across at Bagdemagus.

Bagdemagus looked away quickly.

"He's as bad as a dinner lady!" said Samantha, very shocked, but Simon said no, it was not his fault, his cat food was all gone and he had to keep alive.

"Poor Bagdemagus," said Charlotte. "Don't worry, though! There'll be mustard and cress very soon!"

Bagdemagus shrugged his shoulders but looked slightly comforted. Kate bent down and scooped him up and cuddled him.

"He'll just have to learn to eat grass seeds and beanbags like the rest of us," she said cheerfully. "Come on!"

The grass seeds and beanbags had cooked down (with tapioca of course) into a dark grey lumpy porridge that smelt of old shoes. It was served by Miss Spigot, and even she, hardened dinner lady as she was, was forced to look away as it plopped on to the plates. Class 4b, after three hours hard labour in sub-zero temperatures, ate it quite happily. The grass seeds gave the beans and tapioca a bitter, tangy flavour that people found quite delicious.

"And they are the kiddies that complained about the wrong sort of yoghurt and couldn't be got to eat quiche for love nor money!" marvelled Miss Spigot to Mrs Muldoon and Miss Pilchard over their own late breakfast of pot noodles and cocoa. "Even that cat choked a spoonful down!"

"I've been thinking about that cat," remarked Miss Pilchard. "It would casserole beautiful with a few of those beans and a pinch of grass seed! Haricot Chat au Fine Herbes! I'd eat it myself!"

That morning Simon discovered a perfectly good ground sheet, and Madeline invented a flat-pack igloo that did not need any particular kind of snow.

"Or an expert eskimo!" she said to Dougal McDougal when she erected a display model in the basement for everyone to admire.

Madeline's igloo was made of cardboard boxes. Pudding Bag School had a huge supply of them, stacked up in a corner of the office, waiting to be taken away for recycling. They were the ones that school exercise books were delivered in, and exactly the right size for igloo building.

"But won't they blow away?" asked Kate.

"No, because we will fill them with snow," said Madeline. "And in the mornings all we will have to do is empty them out and fold them flat again and they will be all ready for the next night."

"A flat-pack igloo!" said Dougal. "It's a fantastic idea! Isn't it, Kate?"

Kate said that she supposed it was. She was not at all happy that the expedition was really going to happen, but still, she set about making four sleeping bags. She used black bin bags, lined them with a double layer of red velvet, chopped from the ends of the stage curtains that they slept under at night. When they were finished they were tested on people brought straight from the furthest end of the ice tunnel. Kate was slightly comforted to see that these people turned from pale blue to bright red in a matter of minutes.

"We will be far too hot in them!" grumbled Dougal to Samuel, but he did not say anything to Kate. She was not her usual cheerful self that morning. It was snowing heavily again and she had been up on the roof three times already scraping clear the solar panels. Also she hated sewing at the best of times, but sewing with frost-bitten fingers, after a breakfast of grass seed and beanbag porridge was almost more than she could bear.

Lunch was more grass seed and beanbag porridge, flattened down this time and fried into pancakes. There were two each, and by the time people had chewed their way through their first one they were only too pleased to donate their second to the relief expedition. They were packed with the baby rusks and a few leftover sweets in a couple of backpack-style schoolbags.

"Now all we need is a sledge," said Samuel. They were back in their classroom when he said this. Everyone's eyes roved round the room as he spoke, searching for something large enough and strong enough and flat enough to be made into a sledge. Everyone's gaze seemed to end at Miss Gilhoolie's desk.

It was a beautiful desk. Mr Bedwig had made it before he left, sandpapering and polishing solid pine to the smoothness and glossiness of best quality butterscotch. It was the only desk in the school that did not wobble.

"Solid as a rock," Mr Bedwig had said proudly when he brought it up from the basement. "Brass screws and dovetail joints. Should last for ever!"

"We'll have to get the legs off," said Dougal McDougal. "Let's get it turned over!"

"I can't bear to chop up Miss Gilhoolie's desk," protested Madeline.

"It's by far the best thing in the school to make a sledge from," said Dougal.

"There's other desks."

"Not strong enough. We can't have a sledge that falls to pieces at the first bump. And anyway, we won't be chopping it up, we'll be converting it. It's got to be done!"

Dougal dashed down to the basement and returned with the toolbox. They hacked off the legs, took the fronts off the drawers and used them to make a sort of snowplough arrangement at the front.

"And we can make a harness out of belts or something and fix it to the drawer handles to pull it along," he said.

It took a long time, and a lot of large nails, but it was finished in the end, and then the whole thing was manoeuvred through the trapdoor and down to the basement.

When Kate saw it, wrote Simon in his diary that night, *she said 'Oh Dougal darling!' And other people said other things, some of them very rude, but Madeline went off and started digging at the snow tunnel all by herself.*

Madeline was gone for quite a long time, and when she came back she said, "I've finished it."

There was an immediate stampede, and a few minutes later for the first time for nearly a week, Class 4b stood outside in the open air.

CHAPTER SIX
The Journey North

Samuel Moon woke up very early the next morning with a muddled feeling of terrible gloom. Something bad was about to happen, he was sure, but he could not think what.

And then it came to him.

This was the day when the relief expedition was to set out in search of help.

And one of the relief expedition is me, thought Samuel.

He knew he had only himself to blame. After all, it had been he who discovered the book of Antarctic adventures and read it aloud to the class. He had become the Pudding Bag School Antarctic expert.

But I only ever meant to be the sort of expert who read about things, he thought. Not the sort who did them!

Too late now, Samuel realised. The relief expedition had been thought of, and in a moment of madness he had said that he didn't mind going.

Samuel did what Kate did when she wanted to cheer them up. He crawled quietly out from under his share of the red velvet curtain and lit the beeswax candle. Then he crawled quietly back in again and tried to be brave.

Charlotte and Emma woke up together, as all their lives they had done everything together. Charlotte was to go, and Emma was to stay. Whatever happened in the next few days, whether to Emma left behind in the forgotten school, or to Charlotte on the journey north, nothing would be quite as bad as the fact that one was to go, and one was to stay.

The twins did not say a word to each other, but under the red velvet curtain their hands met together and squeezed.

Bagdemagus uncurled from a red velvet dream and some instinct seemed to tell him that this was the day when his new career as an animated compass would begin. He crept up the basement steps and strengthened himself with a visit to the black-and-white mice.

Madeline opened her eyes and the dim golden light of the beeswax candle was shining all around her. Now that she had to leave it she realised for the first time what a lovely place the basement refuge had been.

Kate woke up saying, "Dougal darling!" and Dougal woke up absolutely jubilant because this was the day when the adventure would begin.

There was no more peace once Dougal was awake. There was nothing but a helter-skelter rush to make sure that the expedition was well on its way before the dinner ladies could do anything to stop it.

They were quickly ready. The four warmest coats had already been chosen, together with gloves and hats and scarves. The two schoolbags of food were packed and waiting, and so was a third one full of spare gloves and hats. The fourth schoolbag was carried by Charlotte. The day before, the mustard and cress plantation had been divided into two. The last schoolbag held the section that was to go with Charlotte. It was to travel in a small greenhouse-style construction made from rulers and plastic bags.

"Well, at least you haven't much to carry," remarked Samantha tactlessly. "And you'll have practically nothing when you've eaten that little bit of food you've got. I wonder if Bagdemagus will really work as a compass cat."

"I'm sure he will," said Madeline, and this was proved a few minutes later when the sledge had been dragged through the tunnel and parked on the snow outside. Bagdemagus, coaxed with great difficulty from the top of the boiler and carried by force into the freezing air outside, pointed at once and most determinedly in the direction of home.

"Poor Bagdemagus!" said Emma.

"Good Bagdemagus!" said Kate, trying to be cheerful. "That's one thing that's working all right already!"

Dougal's sledge was another thing that looked like being a success. Even laden with the flat-pack igloo, sleeping bags and ground sheet it ran at a wonderful speed.

"That's because she always kept it so well polished," remarked Samantha. "She was very proud of it! I remember how pleased she was when Mr Bedwig finished making it."

"Shut up Samantha!" ordered Dougal, seeing Madeline's stricken face. "We had to chop it up! It was a matter of life or death! Anyway, it's just as much use as a sledge as it ever was as a desk!"

"Perhaps one day Mr Bedwig will be able to turn it back into a desk again," said Madeline hopefully.

"If he can get the nails out," said Samantha.

"Shut up, Samantha darling!" said Kate. "Oh, I do wish they didn't have to go! Oh, take no notice of me! I'm sure everything is going to be absolutely all right!"

After that there was a lot of stamping of

cold feet and rubbing of cold fingers and last minute chat about mustard and cress and dinner ladies and how lucky it was that the snow seemed to have stopped for a while.

And then everyone seemed to run out of words. Kate did quite a lot of hugging but nobody cried. Quite suddenly the relief expedition had begun.

They seemed to get far away very quickly, plodding steadily in the direction that everyone agreed looked most like north, over the strange snow-covered landscape of hillocks and bumps that was all that was left of Pudding Bag Lane. They turned around once to wave to those left behind, but that was all. Nobody looked back after that except Bagdemagus.

"I wonder if we'll ever see them again," said Samantha mournfully.

"Breakfast!" exclaimed Kate, and began hurrying people back into the snow tunnel. Most of them went straight away, shivering and slipping and quite glad to get indoors, but Kate and Emma and Simon remained outside. They watched until their feet froze and their eyes streamed with rubbing and staring and rubbing again. They watched until the relief expedition were the size of ants, and the sledge was the size of a dot. And then, between one moment and another they seemed to disappear completely, but Kate and Emma and Simon still watched. And they stood very close together and they did not say a word.

Early mornings were the worst times for the dinner ladies. In the early mornings they never bothered to address each other as 'Dame', and the time when they would be rescued and rewarded for all their hard work seemed very far away. Also they were beginning to run out of all but the plainest of biscuits, and they were getting rather tired of the meals they hotted up for themselves from the bottom of the Emergency Freezer. Not tired enough, of course, for them to think of eating their own cooking instead.

"But we still have to smell it," grumbled Mrs Muldoon as she stirred the morning saucepan full of grass seed and beanbag porridge.

"The fumes seemed to haunt me all night," agreed Amelia Pilchard. "I dreamed of old dogs!"

"And what were the old dogs doing, Amelia dear?" asked Mrs Muldoon nastily.

"Snoring," said Miss Pilchard. "Pass the plates, Pansy, do! Don't just stand there mooning!"

Miss Spigot, instead of passing the plates,

marched angrily out of the kitchen and slammed the door. A few moments later however, she marched back in again, and her voice shook as she spoke.

"Four kiddies short!" she announced. "Did you hear that? We are four kiddies short! They've dug a tunnel and hopped it! That Kate stood there and told me without turning a hair! Whatever shall we do?"

It took some time for Miss Pilchard and Mrs Muldoon to understand. And then they had to rush out and check that it was really true. And then they had to drag from Kate the whole story of the sledge and the escape tunnel and all the other preparations that had gone on under their hard-working and self-sacrificing noses. And then they had to tell Class 4b what they thought of their wicked, devious, ungrateful ways.

This took a long time, so that breakfast

when it finally arrived, was very cold and nasty and stuck to the spoons like glue.

It was a horrible morning at Pudding Bag School.

The reason that the relief expedition disappeared so suddenly from sight was that they sank. The snow looked perfectly solid, but it was not. The snowdrifts had piled and frozen and piled again, but there were air pockets among them, especially around the drifted-over trees. At the end of Pudding Bag Lane the relief expedition plunged seven metres into the arms of an enormous chestnut tree. Nobody was seriously damaged, but it took them most of the morning to clamber back up the snowy branches and out through the topmost twigs into the open air.

"We can't keep doing this," said Charlotte, anxiously inspecting the mustard and cress.

"Some of the stalks have got terribly bent!"

"Let's build the igloo and have a rusk," suggested Dougal, but Madeline said they could not possibly make their first camp at the end of Pudding Bag Lane, and Charlotte and Samuel agreed.

"We've hardly started," said Samuel. "It must be miles and miles yet to the sunny north. Put Bagdemagus back on the sledge, and let's get on."

But Bagdemagus would not get back on the sledge. They had to unpack one of the igloo boxes in the end, and put him in that. And then he was no use at all as an animated compass, because he went round and round in circles, yowling with fury. However they plodded on, and very soon fell into another air pocket.

After this Bagdemagus would not even go near the sledge. He set off in his own direction, and they had no choice but to follow him. Madeline hoped very much that he was not taking them in a circular direction back to Pudding Bag School, but she kept this thought to herself.

"One thing about following Bagdemagus," remarked Dougal, an hour or so later. "We've stopped falling down holes."

It was Madeline and Charlotte's turn to pull the sledge. They grunted, but did not reply. It was beginning to feel very heavy, and the sky was turning a darker and darker blue. Presently they saw a star, and then another, and then Madeline and Samuel made out the Great Bear and Pole star and saw to their relief that they were still going northish, if not absolutely straight north. Bagdemagus continued to stalk on ahead, making wide loops and detours from time to time, always well within sight, but also carefully out of reach. By now they were walking in silence, much too tired to talk.

Another hour passed, and Dougal and Samuel took over the towing. Bagdemagus still would not let himself be caught. Charlotte, without meaning to, suddenly heard herself asking, "Are we nearly there?"

Bagdemagus looked back at her over his shoulder, padded forward a few more steps, and stopped at last.

They built their shelter by moonlight and starlight, scooping snow into the boxes with frozen hands. As soon as a box was filled and closed it was added to the dome-shaped igloo. Madeline hurried round, filling in the cracks with snow. Last of all, the sledge was lifted on to the top to close the final gap in the roof.

It was not until the sledge was in place and packed down with snowballs that Bagdemagus finally allowed himself to be caught.

Inside the igloo it was dark black. Nobody

cared. They spread out the ground sheet,
pulled off their boots, unrolled their sleeping
bags, crawled inside and collapsed.

"What about supper?" asked Dougal, after a
long, long silence, but no one replied. Dougal
fumbled a grass seed and beanbag pancake
out of the schoolbag that he was using for a
pillow, took one bite, and fell asleep before he
had time to take a second.

Back at Pudding Bag School nobody was sleeping very well.

Now the excitement of planning the relief expedition was over, there was nothing to do but wait. It left plenty of time for thinking, and plenty of time for worrying too. Dougal and Madeline, Charlotte and Samuel had left a loneliness behind them when they set off to look for rescue. The basement had lost a lot of its cosiness. Class 4b shivered under the remains of the red velvet curtains. Last and worst of all, Miss Spigot was now sleeping with them to make sure that no more people escaped. Class 4b discovered that Miss Spigot's disagreeable method of soothing herself to sleep was to pull her finger joints until they cracked.

There was nobody in the basement that night who did not envy the relief expedition in their cardboard igloo in the snow.

The relief expedition woke up the next morning to find that they had camped in the shelter of an enormous, snow-covered dome. When they crawled out of the igloo and stamped their feet a strange murmuring ringing filled the air.

They were all four of them enormously happy. The igloo had worked perfectly and their sleeping bags had seemed more comfortable than any beds they had ever known. They had survived a night, and the sky was bright blue and Charlotte said the mustard and cress had grown in the dark.

"Let's climb up to the top of that little hill and see if we can see where we are," suggested Dougal.

Everyone looked at Bagdemagus to see whether this would be allowed, since it was becoming quite clear that he was the real leader of the expedition. Bagdemagus obviously thought it was a good idea. He led the way quite cheerfully, and the hill seemed to whisper under their feet as they climbed.

Something was glinting on the top of the hill, the tip of something metal that shone golden in the sunshine.

"It's a cross," discovered Charlotte, "like on a church."

Madeline gazed at the cross, and at the little round hill they had climbed, and she said wonderingly, "It's the dome of St Paul's!"

And it was.

They ate their pancake breakfast on the top of St Paul's Cathedral, and far away to their left Admiral Nelson kept them company. His column was now a rather short stump, but they were pleased to see that the snowdrift behind it curved exactly like the prow of an enormous ship.

"He looks like he's sailing again," said Samuel.

After breakfast they sledged several times down the dome of St Paul's, because (as Dougal remarked) they would probably never get another chance. Then Bagdemagus took control once more, leading them between half-buried, deserted office blocks. They ate baby rusks for lunch as they walked and endless handfuls of snow to quench their thirst.

Gradually the cheerfulness of the early morning began to wear off. It was very hard going. In some places the snow was so shallow that they stumbled over street lamps, and in others they found themselves skidding on the skylights of buildings buried beneath them. Dougal fell over a radio aerial and hurt his wrist. The sky changed from blue to white, and from white to grey and then suddenly it was snowing very hard indeed.

They hardly had to work to fill the boxes for the igloo that night. They almost filled themselves. Everything was covered in snow very quickly and the snow came with them when they crawled inside. The ground sheet soon became an icy puddle. There was no lying down that night. They sat back to back dozing and chewing on pancakes.

"If we've got to go all the way to Scotland," said Charlotte, "I don't think I can bear it."

Already sledging on the dome of St Paul's seemed a very long time ago.

CHAPTER SEVEN
Howling in the Distance

Each day seems longer than the one before, wrote Simon Percy in his diary.

At Pudding Bag School the waiting was beginning to wear people down. They had not realised, when they planned the relief expedition, how much they would miss them when they were gone.

"I realised," said Emma. "I realised about Charlotte."

Simon, in an effort to replace Samuel, had tried reading aloud Antarctic adventures to Class 4b at night. Somehow, it had not been the same at all.

"I'm sorry, Simon," said Kate. "But it doesn't seem to matter any more."

Dougal and Madeline were terribly missed, natural leaders that they were, and so was Bagdemagus. Even the dinner ladies missed Bagdemagus.

"There was a good two meals on that cat!" said Amelia Pilchard mournfully. "A good two meals and it's walked off into the snow!"

"Try not to take it to heart, Amelia dear," said Mrs Muldoon kindly.

"She's right to be upset," said Miss Spigot, who had been rummaging in the Emergency Freezer while they talked. "I never thought to see the day when the tapioca would run out, and yet run out it has. And the grass seed and beans are just about gone. We'll be down to Rock Bottom before the day's out, which I may as well tell you is Turkey Burgers and Pop

Tarts and a burst bag of peas."

One Bean soup for dinner, wrote Simon in his diary that day. *One Bean soup means you get one bean each, so it wasn't exactly filling but we had mustard and cress for pudding which was very nice indeed.*

He underlined the last sentence and pushed his diary across the table for Emma to read because Kate said Emma needed cheering up. She had been terribly worried by the snowstorm that had begun the night before and she looked up nervously as Kate came in from another session of solar-panel clearing on the roof.

"Stopped at last!" said Kate. "Cheer up Emma! Now perhaps everything will start to come all right!"

The relief expedition knew that the snow had stopped when Bagdemagus scrabbled himself a tunnel and disappeared from the igloo. One by one they followed after him, digging their way out as they went. They found Bagdemagus sitting on a snowdrift, tidying his whiskers. As soon as he saw them he got up and stretched himself, as if just about to go.

"You'll have to wait while we pack our things," Madeline told him. He prowled impatiently around them while they dug first for the sledge and the igloo boxes, and then for their sleeping bags, schoolbags and ground sheet. As soon as they were properly loaded, he set off.

"He seems to know exactly which way he wants to go," observed Charlotte. "I don't know how he can tell. Everything looks the same to me. Do you want to know what I heard last night but I didn't like to tell you in case I frightened you?"

"What?" asked Dougal.

"Howling! Howling like wolves. Far away wolves."

"I expect it was the wind," said Madeline, and Dougal and Samuel agreed.

"It was wolves," said Charlotte stubbornly. "I was really worried about the mustard and cress. Where's Bagdemagus?"

Bagdemagus was far away to their left, a small orange dot in the snow.

"He's definitely taking us somewhere," said Madeline. "I'm sure he is. He's ..."

She broke off suddenly, listening.

"I told you so!" said Charlotte.

It was far, far away but it was undoubtedly wolves.

It was the first sound of life they had heard since they left Pudding Bag School. It caused their hearts to beat faster and their skins to prickle all over with fear.

"Well," said Dougal at last. "We'd better carry on. We can't stay here."

So they set off again, following Bagdemagus.

Something was becoming more and more apparent as they journeyed. The snow was getting less deep. The drifts that had been piled to the height of St Paul's Cathedral were already behind them. It was like travelling from a landscape of snow-peaked mountains, into a country of rolling hills.

"It's hardly as high as the street lamps round here," said Dougal, as if snow as high as street lamps was hardly worth calling snow at all.

"It's still over the doors," said Charlotte, glancing at the buildings on either side. The buildings might as well have been blocks of ice, she thought, for all the use they were, blank-faced and silent and buried to their tightly locked upper windows.

"The doors would probably be locked anyway," said Madeline, and everyone sighed. Something else was becoming obvious, besides the change in depth of the snow. They were travelling in the direction of the wolves.

"I hope Bagdemagus is on our side!" said Charlotte suddenly. "After all, we don't know that he is!"

"Of course he is," said Madeline after a moment's startled silence. "He always has been, hasn't he?"

"I don't know," said Charlotte. "He wasn't very nice about us eating his cat food, was he? And he wouldn't sit on the sledge and be a proper compass cat when we needed him. And now he's taking us in the direction of wolves!"

"Perhaps there's wolves in all directions," suggested Samuel.

That was not a very comforting idea to

think about either.

"Perhaps he's not taking us anywhere at all," said Dougal. "After all, he's just a cat. Perhaps he's just wandering about, like cats do."

"He's not just any old cat!" cried Madeline hotly. "He's special! He's Bagdemagus!"

They paused and looked at Bagdemagus. He was perched on an old brick chimney stack vigourously licking his back end.

"He looks like any old cat to me," said Charlotte sadly.

As the light began to fade they left the streets behind them and came into an open place of hills and hummocks and half-buried trees. Bagdemagus stayed closer now, watching with gleaming eyes and twitching tail as they stumbled and tripped.

"We ought to be thinking about camping for the night," said Madeline, and at that moment the howling, which they had not heard for some time, broke out directly in front of them, and very close indeed.

Charlotte sobbed, and Dougal exclaimed, "Look at Bagdemagus! He's not on our side! He's pleased! He's brought us here on purpose and he's pleased!"

Dougal was right, Bagdemagus, springing jauntily ahead of them as if hurrying to greet the hidden wolves, looked very pleased indeed. He disappeared over a ridge of snow, and the wolf voices sang louder than ever.

And then Madeline shouted, "Look!"

Bagdemagus came bounding back with twelve wolves behind him and everyone sighed with enormous relief because the twelve wolves were in double file and harnessed to a sleigh.

"It's Mr Bedwig!" said Madeline, and it was.

Mr Bedwig was short and fat with white hair

and spectacles. He looked exactly the sort of person who would spend a hard winter dozing in front of a fire with a crossword puzzle. But Mr Bedwig had hidden talents, and school caretaking and rocket building were just the beginning of them. His ancestors had been caretakers in the Ark, and handiness with animals ran in his family. So did coping with emergencies without any fuss and not being upset by a bit of weather. There was no one in the world, thought Madeline, quite like Mr Bedwig.

There was no one in the world she would rather have met just then.

"Now then Madeline Brown and Co," said Mr Bedwig, bringing his wolf team and sleigh to a tidy halt as he spoke. "Whatever have you been up to with that poor old cat of mine?"

The relief expedition rushed to explain.

"Oh, Mr Bedwig!"

"Oh, Mr Bedwig!"

"Oh, Mr Bedwig!"

"Never mind the Oh Mr Bedwigging!" interrupted Mr Bedwig. "These wolves won't stand for ever! You get on and explain!"

"We had to bring Bagdemagus. We were afraid the dinner ladies might cook him if we didn't."

"They've already cooked the office goldfish, and the stick insects."

"Yes, and gerbil kebabs!"

"We had dinner ladies' detention; we were snowed up for days!"

"We've been living in the basement. We escaped through your passage."

"They're all still there, the rest of our class, and the dinner ladies and Kate."

"They've only got grass seeds and beanbags to eat. That's all they've had for days."

"And mustard and cress."

"We've been out for three days with a cardboard box igloo."

"We dug a huge tunnel and Kate made us sleeping bags."

"Bagdemagus was a compass cat. He brought us to you."

"We're terribly, terribly sorry about Miss Gilhoolie's desk."

"Well I never!" said Mr Bedwig, seeming to be quite bowled over by this flood of information. "Well I never, never did! Clever old Puss! And now I think the lot of you had best come back with me."

"Back where?" asked Dougal, Charlotte and Samuel, but Madeline knew the answer already. Kate had told them long ago. Before any of this had started. Mr Bedwig had been left in charge of the cold weather animals. They were going back to the zoo.

There was room on the sleigh for everyone with the sledge (at which Mr Bedwig tutted but made no comment) tied on behind. "Now no pushing or loud talk," he warned. "I've got the reindeer trained to pull as gentle as lambs but these are pure-bred Siberian wolves and they excite very easily!"

Charlotte clutched Bagdemagus tightly at this remark.

"They haven't been getting the exercise they should," explained Mr Bedwig. "What with having to take turns with the reindeer and moose! And I can't turn them loose on account of the penguins ..."

Samuel gave a huge yawn and suddenly nodded forward.

"Not to mention the polars who've no patience at all ..."

As patient as polars, thought Madeline drowsily. On account of the penguins ... Pure-bred Siberian ... don't get the exercise ...

Madeline was asleep and Samuel was asleep.
Charlotte's head tipped further and further
forward until it came to rest on Bagdemagus's
furry gold coat, and it was like tilting into a
dream. Dougal, swaying from side to side with
the motion of the sleigh said, "I'm jolly well
not ... going to slee ... like they have ..." and
came to rest against Mr Bedwig's broad
shoulder and did not speak again.

Mr Bedwig's winter home was the old Keeper's
Lodge at the zoo. From there he had
constructed a series of ice tunnels leading in
all directions, to the penguins' frozen lake, the
wolf dens, the reindeer stables and polar-bear
enclosure, all buried under the snow. Further
tunnels led to the surface, so that the animals
could be properly exercised and to the zoo
warehouses, where vast supplies of food, both

human and animal were stored away.

"A place for everything and everything in its place," remarked Mr Bedwig as he unloaded his sleeping passengers at the Keeper's Lodge and drove his wolf team away to be rubbed down and fed.

In the Keeper's Lodge the relief expedition slept and slept. Ages and ages later they woke up to the smell of sausages and baked potatoes, and found themselves tucked up in a tidy line on the floor with rugs and cushions. Through an open door they could see Mr Bedwig lifting dishes from an oven and carrying them to a table, sausages, baked potatoes, rice pudding and apple pie.

"How long have we been asleep?" asked Madeline.

"A day and a night," said Mr Bedwig. "Or rather, a night and a day. I don't know what you might call this meal, breakfast or supper, but it's ready when you are!" And he plonked a jug of hot chocolate in the middle of the table.

Madeline, Dougal, Samuel and Charlotte looked at the hot chocolate. Then they looked at each other, and they thought of Kate and Simon and all their friends eating grass seed and beanbag porridge in the gloomy dining room of Pudding Bag School.

"Mr Bedwig," said Madeline. "Do you think it would keep hot?"

At Pudding Bag School at suppertime Kate said that she was not hungry, and Mrs Muldoon said, "Suit yourself," and Kate went out on to the roof.

It was nearly dark, but no stars shone. A tear trickled down Kate's nose as she thought of the supper going on in the school below, cold bean salad and grass-seed soup. Another tear fell as she remembered the anxious face of

Emma as she bent over the last of the mustard and cress. Then a whole shower of tears for Dougal, Madeline, Samuel and Charlotte far away in the snow. And then, on the wind, came a sound that stopped Kate's tears like magic.

Sleigh bells.

Sleigh bells coming closer and closer.

The journey that had taken the relief expedition nearly three days was retraced in less than an hour. Mr Bedwig and Bagdemagus led the way with the wolf sleigh, and Charlotte and Dougal followed behind driving nine reindeer and a moose.

"Can't take you all," Mr Bedwig had warned, and Samuel and Madeline, realising that extra sausages and potatoes would be needed, had volunteered to stay behind and cook.

Once again they steered by Bagdemagus,

but this time he rode instead of marching ahead, and all the way his nose pointed unwaveringly in the direction of home. They passed out of the empty park and through the silent streets, skirted the dome of St Paul's and headed due south to Pudding Bag Lane and Kate, standing among the snowy roof peaks, with tears drying on her cheeks.

CHAPTER EIGHT
What Happened In The End

The sound of the sleigh bells, mingled with Kate's shrieks of joy, penetrated down to the dining room where Class 4b were gathered.

In no time at all the room was empty. They raced through the classrooms and down to the basement, tore along the passage and burst out of the tunnel into the open air. Then for a few minutes there was a most joyful reunion in the snow.

"You'll catch your deaths-a-cold," said Mr Bedwig in the end, when the hugging and exclaiming showed signs of ending.

"Go and wrap up warm and come straight back! No you can't stroke the doggies, Young Lady! They are pure-bred Siberian wolves and excite very easily! Hurry up the lot of you! And don't forget those blessed dinner ladies that I've heard so much about!"

They were ready in a very few minutes, and they did not forget the dinner ladies, who came over "All sudden jelly" as Mrs Muldoon put it, at the news of rescue at last. The guinea pigs, gerbils and black-and-white mice were

stowed in Mr Bedwig's pockets and the two sleighs were packed.

"A tight squeeze," remarked Mr Bedwig. "But I daresay it would have been tighter a week ago. Anyway, we'll soon have you there."

"Dougal darling," said Kate, a few minutes later. "Ought you to drive so very, very fast?"

"Yes I ought," replied Dougal, slapping the reins up and down vigourously as he spoke. "Madeline and Samuel are cooking supper. Sausages, baked potatoes, rice pudding and apple pie!"

A day or two later the dinner ladies had recovered completely and had settled down at the zoo as if they had lived there all their lives. They had also grown very fond of Mr Bedwig.

"He's a very gallant old gent!" said Mrs

Muldoon over breakfast one morning.

Miss Spigot and Miss Pilchard nodded in kindly agreement. There was no denying Mr Bedwig's gallantry. He had rescued them when they were down to their last three turkey burgers and had almost lost all hope. He had given up the Keeper's Lodge for them and moved uncomplainingly into the monkey house instead. He had taken over responsibility for Class 4b, and last, and best of all, he refused to allow them to cook. He said they had done enough and the dinner ladies quite agreed.

Class 4b were also living in the monkey house, two or three to a cage and very comfortable indeed. They spent their time helping to take care of the cold weather animals (fourteen wolves, nine reindeer, one moose, two polar bears and forty-two penguins) and learning to cook. The time passed very quickly and happily and there was great disappointment when the Great Thaw began and the snow tunnels linking the cages began to collapse and green grass appeared for the first time in weeks.

The Great Thaw was followed by south-west gales and a heat wave which was very useful because it meant that the melting snowdrifts disappeared almost instantly instead of causing floods. In a remarkably short time London was back to normal again, and Class 4b went home to their loving families, who all the time had believed them to be living happily in a remote Scottish castle, not bothering to write.

And so Pudding Bag School, returned to its usual quiet life.

The dinner ladies did not. The story of their nobleness impressed the nation. They were given Damehoods and lifelong pensions and featured in a documentary on Prime-Time TV.

They never went back to cooking.

Dame Amelia became a fortune teller and Dame Lacey a chat-show host and Dame Pansy wrote a best-selling book called COPING WITH THE KIDDIES which was later made into a film. White marble statues were erected to all three of them in Regent's Park and Pudding Bag School had a day off for the unveiling.

There were crowds and cheering and thousands of flowers, wrote Simon Percy in his diary that night. *And their names were carved at the bases of each statue:*

Dame Lacey Muldoon
Dame Pansy Spigot
Dame Amelia Pilchard

I think they were pleased, wrote Simon.

At Pudding Bag School the missing stick insects
and gerbils and black-and-white mice were
soon replaced, and Mr Bedwig repaired Miss
Gilhoolie's desk so that it was as good as new.
Bagdemagus continued to live with them,
spending most of his days asleep in patches of
sunlight, but always waking in time to share the
packed lunches that people now brought
instead of school dinners.

"He's a very good cat," said Dougal
McDougal.

"He's the best cat in the world," said
Madeline Brown.

More Pudding Bag School adventures:

97S 0 340 97017 1

978 0 340 97030 0

A Strong Smell of Magic

CHAPTER ONE

Class 4b, Pudding Bag School, were taught to recognise the smell of magic by their teacher, Miss Gilhoolie. She thought it was very important.

A lot of people did not know what to think of Miss Gilhoolie. She seemed too cheerful for a teacher, and too pretty. She was very fond of diamonds (the bigger the better) and she wore them every day by the dozen. Her shiny bright green Ferrari also surprised people, and so did the way she could whistle through her fingers, and so did her short, tight skirts.

Class 4b thought she was a very good teacher.

"She may be bossy," said Dougal McDougal. "But at least she is not boring!"

169

Dougal McDougal was ten years old. He had red hair and lots of ideas, not all of them very good. His best friend was Simon Percy. Simon also had ideas, less than Dougal, but usually better. Simon was much quieter than Dougal, but then so was everyone else in Class 4b.

There were two classes of ten year olds in Pudding Bag School: 4a and 4b.

"Class 4a is the brainy ones' class!" said Class 4a. "Class 4b are all nutters! And Miss Gilhoolie is the nuttiest of all!"

"You're just jealous," said Dougal McDougal.

Miss Gilhoolie had a way of making lessons interesting. Science included popcorn making and panning for gold. The Geography Project survey was done by hot-air balloon. Class 4b's lessons were so unusual that none of them were surprised when they heard that 4b would not be joining any of the other classes on the school summer trip.

All the other classes were going to visit zoos and adventure playgrounds and open-air theatres.

"Very nice indeed," said Miss Gilhoolie to Class 4b. "We would do the same if only we could spare the time. Our class trip will be Purely Educational. Pass round these letters to parents, please Madeline, and make sure you all bring them back signed in the morning."

Class 4b grabbed the letters as Madeline handed them out and read them eagerly. Then they looked at each other in dismay. It seemed like the Class 4b school summer trip was going to be far from exciting.

This is what the letters said:

Dear Parent/Guardian,

We hope your son/daughter will be able to join us on our annual summer trip. To keep costs to a

minimum each student will need to bring a packed lunch,
water bottle, and snacks for the journey. A small
donation towards the cost of travel (not more than
£3.00) would be appreciated but is not essential.

NB School uniform MUST be worn and (as usual)
PLEASE no fizzy drinks!

Guinevere Gilhoolie

Please return the attached slip:

I give consent for -------------- (name of student) to take
part in the summer class trip (A Practical
Demonstration of the Smell of Magic)

I do/do not enclose a donation towards the cost of
travel (please state amount)---------
Signed:------------------(Parent/Guardian)

"But does magic smell?" asked Simon Percy
(who was rather sorry to be missing the

adventure playgrounds).

"Of course it does," said Miss Gilhoolie.
"Everyone has smelt it, sometime or another.
The trouble is that most people do not
recognise it, which is a waste because it is
there for a reason."

"What reason?" asked Madeline Brown (who
would have loved to visit an open-air theatre).

"To warn you not to meddle," said Miss
Gilhoolie, "and also (of course) to remind you
to enjoy yourself. It is very important that you
learn to recognise it and that is why we are
going on this class trip."

"But how are we going to find magic to
smell?" asked Samantha Freebody (who
would have liked very much to go to the zoo).
"What if we can't? It will be a complete waste
of time!"

"Unless Miss Gilhoolie can do magic
herself," suggested Dougal, cheerfully. "Can

you do magic, Miss Gilhoolie?"

"Really Dougal, do I look like a witch?" demanded Miss Gilhoolie, and then just as Dougal was about to reply "Yes, very much," went on, "Of course, I can't conjure up the exact smell of real magic, but what I have arranged for you is a very good second best. It is often used for training purposes. Copy down this recipe in the backs of your Science and Technology books."

The recipe was:

One large bottle of the most expensive French perfume

One large healthy hedgehog

One large barrow-load of freshly fallen snow (preferably taken from a pine forest)

One boot cupboard full of well-worn old boots

A fresh west wind off the sea

"Those are the standard ingredients," said Miss Gilhoolie, briskly. "And anything else is fiddle-faddle! Yes, Simon dear?"

"Does it hurt the hedgehog?"

"Of course it does not hurt the hedgehog!" said Miss Gilhoolie. "You merely add the hedgehog to the boots, wait two minutes to allow the smell to infuse, pile in the snow (it will not bother the hedgehog at all as long as we brush it off again before it melts), pour on the perfume, and open all the windows so that the wind blows through. And there you are!"

"I should think," remarked Madeline Brown, who was very clever, "that you must have to be very quick. Otherwise, won't the snow melt and the hedgehog run away and the boots and the perfume get too strong to bear?"

"Timing is absolutely critical," agreed Miss Gilhoolie. "Now, it is a long way from here to a suitable coast with a reliable west wind from the sea, so I am afraid the coach will not be able to wait for anyone who is late. I have hired an understanding fisherman's cottage,

and the snow is being flown in from Norway
by a friend of mine and will reach us at twelve
o'clock. We will leave school at eight in the
morning and there should just be time for one
good sniff each before we have to come back.
Any more questions?"

"It seems an awful lot of trouble," said
Samantha Freebody.

"It will be worth it," said Miss Gilhoolie.

Just after twelve o'clock the next day Class
4b, rather stiff after their three and a half hour
coach ride, filed one by one into the
understanding fisherman's cottage, stuck their
heads into the boot cupboard where the
ingredients had been mixed, breathed deeply,
said "Oh Miss Gilhoolie!" breathed again, and
then filed out and back on to the coach for the
long journey back home.

And all of them agreed that it had been
worth it.